The Elephant and the Sea

Ed Vere

In a village by the sea,
carved into the rockiest edge of land,
where the waves are wild and tumbling . . .

lives an old elephant.

His name is Gabriel.

Milou, the sea cat, purrs by his side.

Gabriel's face has as many lines as the sea has waves.
His knees crack. His back creaks.

He sits in the harbor, watching life go by,
thinking about the old days.

Many years ago, before you were born,

when he was a young elephant . . .

In those days, young Gabriel
      ran down to the sea every morning.

Past the boatbuilders, building.
Past the net menders, mending.
Past the sailmakers, stitching.

Gabriel ran past them all,
until he got to the thing he loved
most in all the world . . .

. . . the lifeboat!

Gabriel loved to see the crew at work,
making the lifeboat shipshape.

He wanted to be brave like them—
 rowing into danger, helping sailors in trouble at sea,
singing as they went,
 "Heave away, haul away, heave-HO!"

One day Gabriel asked,
"Can I join you?"

"You're a bit young, my boy.
Come back when you're older.
Come back when you're stronger."

"I will!" said Gabriel.

So Gabriel went away.
He read books about wild seas,
    ferocious storms, and daring rescues.

He practiced rowing.

"Heave away, haul away, heave-HO!"

He grew older.
He grew stronger . . .

He grew bigger.

Gabriel asked again,
"Can I join you?"

"Oh, Gabriel, you've grown a bit!
You're too big for the boat!
We're sorry."

Heave-ho.
Oh no.

At home, Gabriel stared far out to sea
and heaved a long sigh.

He watched the rolling waves
and thought an important thought.

There is only one thing I want to do . . .

So I will do it!

Gabriel made a plan.

Day after day,
　　along the beach,
　　　　he collected driftwood.

Night after night, he worked.
He hammered, he sawed,
he painted, and he sang.

"*Heave away, heave-HO!*"

BANG
BANG BANG

Summer turned to autumn.

One bright winter morning,
gulls were seen far out to sea.
Which meant fish!

The day held the promise
        of an almighty catch.

*"Fish ahoy, my hearties.
        Heave away, haul away,
                heave-HO!"*

Wind filled their sails,
        and the fleet set out.

But the day turned sour.
          Storm clouds glowered.
Thunder rumbled,
          lightning struck.
The wind whipped and whistled.

The waves turned into giants,
          tumbling, lashing, and crashing.

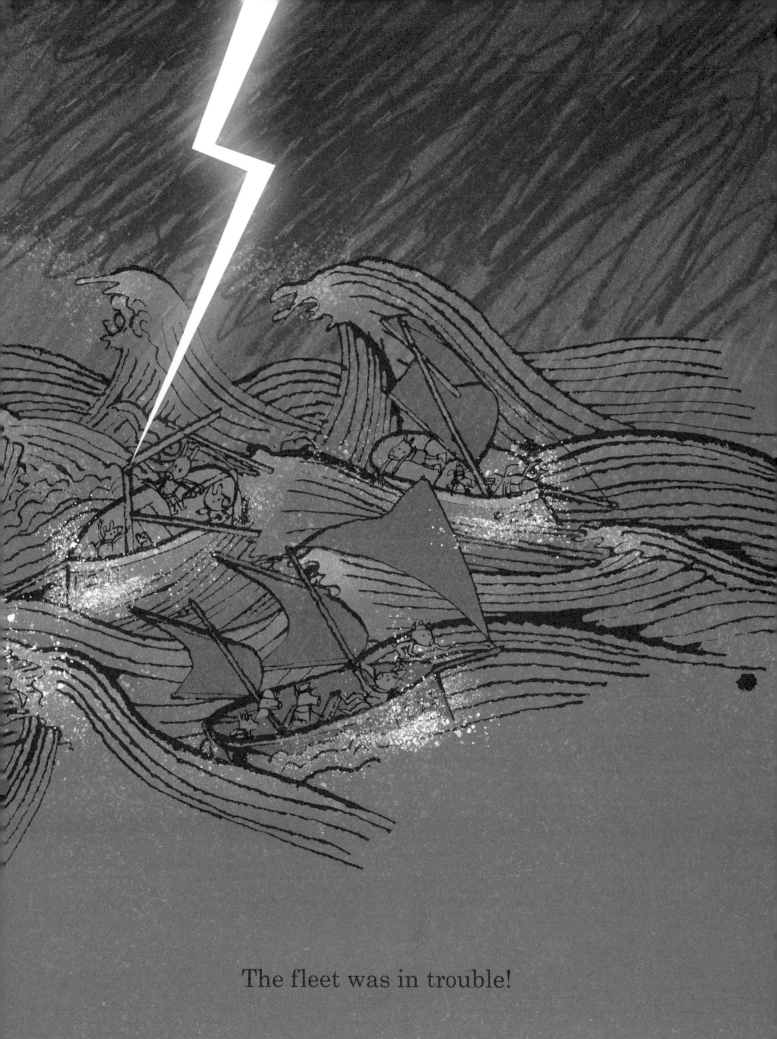

The fleet was in trouble!

The alarm sounded.
The lifeboat launched.

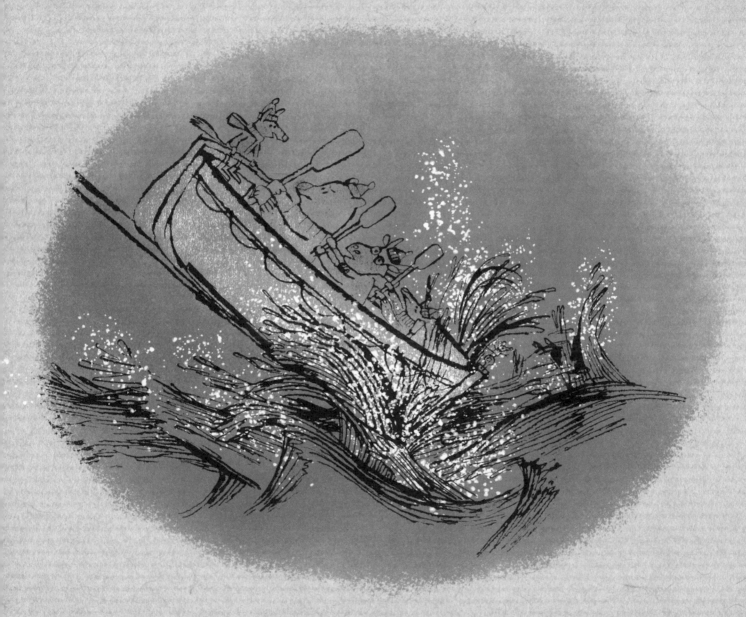

The crew rowed with all their might.

*"Heave away,
haul away,
heave-ho and ROW!"*

But no . . . oh no!
They were not strong enough
to battle this giant sea.

All hope was lost.

But wait! Here's Gabriel!

He had built a boat.
Built for strength. Built for him!

Brave Gabriel rowed out
through thundering waves.
Strong as oak, he pulled the oars.

*"Heave away,
haul away,
heave-ho, heave-HO!"*

Each stroke was hard,
but Gabriel was determined.

In the middle of the crashing waves,
Gabriel found the fleet!

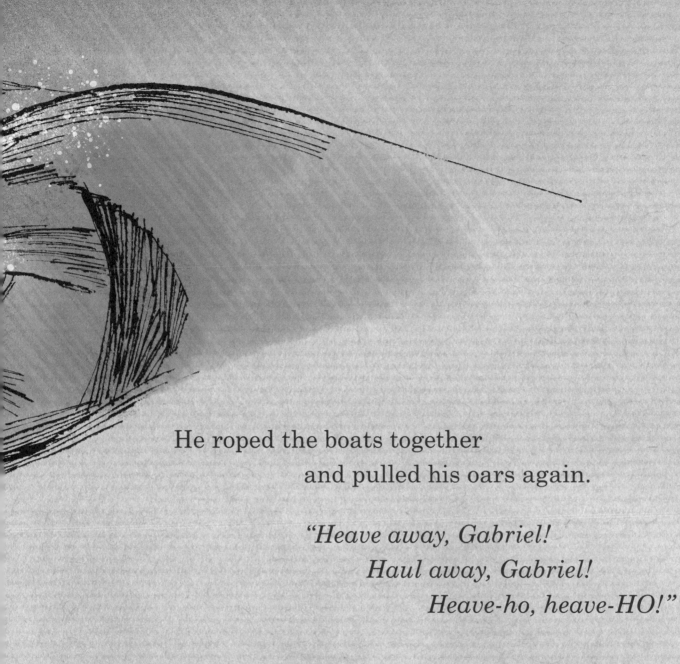

He roped the boats together
and pulled his oars again.

"Heave away, Gabriel!
Haul away, Gabriel!
Heave-ho, heave-HO!"

He towed the fleet to safety.
He towed them safely home.

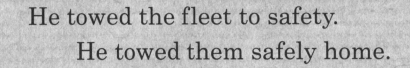

"Brave Gabriel, our hero!"

"Can *we* join *you*?"
                    asked the lifeboat crew.

"Of course!" said Gabriel.
"But we might need a bigger boat."

All together, they hammered, they sawed,
they painted, and they sang.

"Heave away, haul away,
heave-ho, heave-HO!"

They built a new boat.
A strong boat . . .

A boat big enough for everyone.

And so Gabriel lived a life he loved.
Part of the crew, saving sailors at sea.

And today, many years later, here sits Gabriel.
Happy in his old sea boots.
Milou, the sea cat, purrs by his side.

Not everyone knows how brave he has been.

But we do.

> *So heave away, my hearties!*
> *Haul away, my loves!*
> *Heave-ho, HEAVE-HO!*

This book is set in the wild and beautiful land of Cornwall, where I lived
for a winter. One cold, blustery day I sat on a cliff, somewhere between Falmouth
and Mousehole, and painted the village below. That painting is the first picture
in this book. That village is where I first saw Gabriel. He was very old and
he told me the story of his life. This book is his story.

Ed Vere

This book is dedicated to my Grandpa, who sailed the seven seas.
With thanks to Andrea MacDonald and Goldy Broad for making this voyage with me.

Copyright © 2024 by Ed Vere
All rights reserved. Published in the United States by Doubleday, an imprint of Random House Children's Books,
a division of Penguin Random House LLC, New York.
Simultaneously published in slightly different form in the United Kingdom by Puffin Books, London, in 2023.
DOUBLEDAY YR with colophon is a registered trademark of Penguin Random House LLC.
Visit us on the Web! rhcbooks.com
Educators and librarians, for a variety of teaching tools, visit us at RHTeachersLibrarians.com
Library of Congress Cataloging-in-Publication Data
Name: Vere, Ed, author. | Title: The elephant and the sea / Ed Vere. | Description: First edition. |
New York : Doubleday Books for Young Readers, 2024. | Audience: Ages 3–7. |
Summary: Gabriel the elephant reminisces on his younger days and his dreams of being a member of a brave lifeboat crew.
Identifiers: LCCN 2023024911 (print) | LCCN 2023024912 (ebook) |
ISBN 978-0-525-58090-4 (trade) | ISBN 978-0-525-58091-1 (lib. bdg.) | ISBN 978-0-525-58092-8 (ebook)
Subjects: CYAC: Elephants—Fiction. | Lifeboats—Fiction. |
Rescue work—Fiction. | LCGFT: Animal fiction. | Picture books.
Classification: LCC PZ7.V586 El 2024 (print) | LCC PZ7.V586 (ebook) | DDC [E]—dc23

MANUFACTURED IN CHINA
10 9 8 7 6 5 4 3 2 1 First American Edition

Doubleday Books for Young Readers

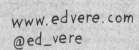

www.edvere.com
@ed_vere

With thanks to all the brave people
who risk their lives to save others.

You can find out how to
support lifeboat crews at

rnli.org